www.enchantedlion.com

First English-language edition published in 2018 by Enchanted Lion Books
67 West Street, 317A, Brooklyn, NY 11222
Orignally published in Sweden as "Koko and Bosse"
Copyright © 2011 by Lisen Adbåge and Natur & Kultur
Published by Agreement with Koja Agency
Copyright © 2018 for the English-language translation by Annie Prime
Copyright © 2018 for the English-language edition by Enchanted Lion Books
ISBN 978-1-59270-258-9

Printed in China by RR Donnelley Asia Printing Solutions Ltd.

1 3 5 7 9 10 8 6 4 2

Lisen Adbåge

TRANSLATED FROM SWEDISH BY ANNIE PRIME

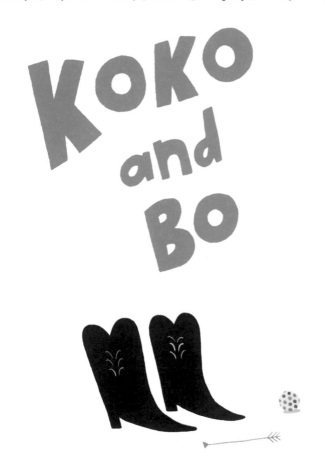

KOKO and BO

ENCHANTED LION BOOKS
NEW YORK

Koko and Bo are at the playground.
They have been there for four hours.

"Time to go home!" says Bo.

"I DON'T WANT TO!" says Koko.

"Don't then," says Bo.

It is dark by the time the doorbell rings.
It is Koko.

Koko wants to come in.
It was boring staying out alone.

"Do you want a sandwich?" asks Bo.

They eat their bedtime snacks
and do crossword puzzles.

"Time for bed, off you go!" says Bo.

"I DON'T WANT TO!" says Koko.

"Stay here then," says Bo.

Koko stays in the kitchen stubbornly for 15 whole minutes.
Bo has fallen right to sleep and is snoring loudly.
It sounds cozy.
Koko tiptoes in and snuggles into bed next to Bo.

"Goodnight little Koko," whispers Bo.

The following day is sunny.
Bo wakes up first.

"It's morning. Time to get up!"

"I DON'T WANT TO!" says Koko.

"Stay in bed then," says Bo.

The clock strikes one. Then three.
Then half past four.
The oatmeal gets cold.
Bo has had time to clean and do laundry
and water the flowers.

"I am about to clear away the breakfast," says Bo.

"No, wait. I want some!" Koko gets up and wolfs down the
 oatmeal in five seconds.
 Luckily, Bo had warmed it up in the microwave.
 It was boring lying in bed.
 Koko got hungry, too.

"Now we are going out to get groceries.
 Put your raincoat on," says Bo.

"I DON'T WANT TO!" says Koko.

"Forget it then," says Bo.

Koko is shivering as Bo locks up his bicycle.

"Brrr," says Koko.

"Here, I brought an extra sweater," says Bo.

The store is big and packed with people.

"Sit here in the shopping cart so you don't wander off," says Bo.

"I DON'T WANT TO!" says Koko.

"Ok, then," says Bo.

Soon there is an announcement over the loudspeaker
saying that Koko has wandered off and is waiting
in the checkout area.

Bo finishes his shopping and goes to get Koko.

"What do you have there?" says Bo. "Hats and marshmallows?"

"MINE," says Koko.

"But you have to pay for them," says Bo.

"I DON'T WANT TO!" says Koko.

"No, well, okay, fine," says Bo.

The store alarm goes off and two guards appear.

"You have to pay for those!" says one of the guards.

"BUT I DON'T WANT TO!" says Koko.

"Then there will be no hats or marshmallows for you!" says the other guard.

Koko has to put everything back.

"Time to go home," says Bo. "Up you get!"

When they cycle past the playground Koko points and says:

"Stop, stop!"

"I DON'T WANT TO!" says Bo. "I want to go home and eat marshmallows."

"Yay!" says Koko.

(Luckily, Bo had already bought the marshmallows.)